P9-DEA-895

In a high-rise building
deep in the heart of a big city
live two private eyes:
Bunny Brown and Jack Jones.
Bunny is the brains,
Jack is the snoop,
and together they
crack cases wide open.

This is the story of
Case Number 008:
THE CASE OF
THE DESPERATE DUCK.

story by
Cynthia Rylant

pictures by
G. Brian Karas

Acrylic, gouache, and pencil were used for the full-color art.
The text type is Times.

Library of Congress Cataloging-in-Publication Data
Rylant, Cynthia.
The high-rise private eyes: the case of the desperate duck /
by Cynthia Rylant, pictures by G. Brian Karas.
    p.   cm.
"Greenwillow Books."
Summary: In their latest case, animal detectives Bunny and Jack help
Mabel the duck find out who stole the sugar cubes from her tea room.
ISBN 0-06-053451-6 (trade). ISBN 0-06-053452-4 (lib. bdg.)
[1. Animals—Fiction. 2. Mystery and detective stories.] I. Title:
Case of the desperate duck. II. Karas, G. Brian, ill.
PZ7.R982Hoe 2005 [E]—dc22 2004010870

First Edition 10 9 8 7 6 5 4 3

Greenwillow Books

Contents

Chapter 1
Popsicles

One day Bunny and Jack
were putting together a puzzle
in Jack's apartment.
"This is hard," said Jack.
"It's supposed to be hard," said Bunny.
"But it's a brown pyramid
in a brown desert," said Jack.
"Right," said Bunny.

"Oh, then I guess I need
a BROWN puzzle piece," said Jack.
"Hmmm. Where can I find one?
Oh, look, here are a MILLION of them!"
"Very funny, Jack," said Bunny.

"Marbles would be more fun," said Jack.

"If you hadn't lost yours," said Bunny.

"But I never had any marbles," said Jack.

"Exactly," said Bunny.

"Am I missing something here?"
asked Jack.

Bunny sighed.

"You're right, Jack," she said.

"Brown is boring.

Let's do something else."

"Goody," said Jack.

"Let's go to my place
   and get Popsicles," said Bunny.
"Okay," said Jack.
"But I'm not eating
   on the balcony."
"Okay," said Bunny.

"I'm not even going to look
out the window," said Jack.
"Okay," said Bunny.
"I might not even open my eyes at all,"
said Jack.

"OH, FOR HEAVEN'S SAKE!"

said Bunny.

"Just come up for a Popsicle!"

"Okay, okay," said Jack.

"Only if I get grape."

"Grape it is," said Bunny.

"If I get dizzy then I get orange, too,"

said Jack.

"*Okay!* Let's go," said Bunny.

They went to Bunny's apartment
on the twenty-second floor.
Bunny looked in the freezer.
"I can't believe I'm out of Popsicles,"
said Bunny.
"Who ate them all?" asked Jack.
"Let's see," said Bunny. "As I recall
it was you, you, you, and you."
"Oh," said Jack.

"Well, you made me watch

all those sewing videos.

I can't watch sewing without a Popsicle.

Several of them.

In fact, *nonstop* Popsicles."

"Okay, okay," said Bunny.

"I have an idea.

Let's go for high tea."

"Can't," said Jack. "Afraid of heights."

"Very funny," Bunny said.

"But you'll get lots of cookies."

"Really?" asked Jack.

"And sandwiches," said Bunny.

"Really?" asked Jack.

"And you get to drink
out of a fancy flowered teacup,"
said Bunny.
"You said cookies, right?" asked Jack.
"Let's go," said Bunny.

Chapter 2
The Case

At Mabel's Tea Room
high tea was in full swing.
All the tables had fancy tablecloths
and fancy teapots
and plates full of fancy cookies
and sandwiches.

"Wow," said Jack. "Fancy."

"It's fun," said Bunny.

"Cookies are always fun," said Jack.

A white duck with pink earrings
waved to them.

"Hello, hello!" she said.

"Welcome to Mabel's Tea Room."

"Thanks," said Jack. "Cool place."

"I'm Mabel. Let me take you to your table," said the duck.

Jack looked at Bunny.

Bunny looked at Jack.

"Not a word, Jack," said Bunny.

"Okay, Bunny, I won't be funny," said Jack.

"Ugh," said Bunny.

They followed Mabel to a table.

Then Mabel left to fix their tea.

"Cookies and rhyming," said Jack.

"I love high tea."

"Ooh," said Bunny.

"Cucumber sandwiches."

"Really?" said Jack. "Let me try."

Jack took a bite.

"Ooh," said Jack. "High tea is fun."

Suddenly,

"EEEEEEEEK!" came a scream.

"Heavens!" said Bunny.

"Yikes!" said Jack.

The scream came from Mabel

at the tea counter.

Bunny and Jack ran over to her.

"What's wrong?" asked Jack.

"Can we help?" asked Bunny.

"I just ran out of cubes.

   And my extra box is missing!"

   cried Mabel.

"You're screaming

   about running out of sugar?" asked Jack.

"I thought only I did that."

"You don't understand," said Mabel.
"My mother is coming to visit,
and fancy sugar cubes
are her favorite part
of high tea!"

25

Mabel fluttered her wings.

"I can't disappoint my mother!" she wailed.

Jack looked at Bunny.

"She can't disappoint her mother," said Jack.

Bunny pulled out her notepad.

"Ma'am, we are private detectives,"
said Bunny.

"Who appreciate sugar," said Jack.

Chapter 3
Cubes

Bunny and Jack

sat back down at their table.

They looked at their clues.

"Okay," said Bunny.

"The extra box of sugar cubes

is missing."

"Right," said Jack.

"The box was on the bottom shelf
of the tea counter," said Bunny.
"Right," said Jack.
"And there are no suspects,"
said Bunny.
"Well, everybody who likes sugar,"
said Jack.

"Yes," said Bunny.

"But whoever took these cubes
  didn't want plain sugar.
  They wanted cubes."

"Cubes are cute, that's why," said Jack.

"Yes, but . . . ," said Bunny.

"I mean, you can eat them
  or you can play with them," said Jack.

"Yes, but . . . but, wait!" said Bunny.

"You're right! Maybe whoever took them
didn't need sugar.
Maybe whoever took them
needed cubes."
"Who needs cubes?" asked Jack.
"I don't know," said Bunny. "Yet."

"Maybe we should hang around
  and look for suspects," said Jack.
"Good idea," said Bunny.
"Gee," said Jack,
"how will I ever pass the time?
  Oh, let's see, sandwiches!
  And cookies! Ooh, little pink cookies!"
"Just watch everybody," said Bunny.
"I'm watching," said Jack.
"Do I have crumbs around my nose?"

Bunny and Jack watched everybody
who went in and out
of Mabel's Tea Room.
They didn't see anybody
who looked like somebody
who needed sugar cubes.
Then two ferrets walked out.
"Look," said Bunny.

"Look at what?" asked Jack.

"Just look," said Bunny.

"Oh," said Jack. "Bingo."

"Let's follow them," said Bunny.
Bunny and Jack followed the ferrets
into the fabric shop next door.

"Play it cool," said Bunny.

"Right," said Jack.

"May I help you?"

the big ferret suddenly asked them.

"We are NOT following you!" said Jack.

"Jack!" said Bunny.

"Oops," said Jack. "Forgot."

The ferret looked confused.

"Is this your shop, sir?" asked Bunny.

"It is," said the ferret.

"I am Louis and this is my son, Louis Jr.

May I help you?"

"It's a wonderful shop," said Bunny.

"Such nice fabric."

"Thank you," said the ferret.

"I love to sew," said Bunny.

"She loves to sew," said Jack.

"I'd like to sew something for an Eskimo doll,"
   said Bunny.

"I know all about Eskimos!" said Louis Jr.

"You do?" asked Bunny.

The little ferret held up his book.

"See?" he said.

"Right," said Bunny.

"I bet you even know how

to make an igloo."

"I do!" said Louis Jr.

"I even made one for school!"

"You did?" asked Bunny.

"I bet you made it out of peanut butter,"
said Jack.

"No, I didn't," said Louis Jr.

"Baking soda," said Jack.

"No," said Louis Jr.

"Sprinkles," said Jack.

"No," said Louis Jr.

"Mabel's sugar cubes," said Bunny.

Louis Jr. looked at Bunny.

"Uh-oh," he said.

Louis Fabrics

Chapter 4
Solved

Louis Jr. took what was left
of Mabel's sugar cubes
back to the Tea Room.
(There were still enough
for Mabel's mother.)

Louis Jr. told Mabel he was sorry
he took the cubes.
"I just needed a good grade,"
said Louis Jr.
"I'm flunking reading."

Mabel was a duck with a good heart.
So she told Louis Jr.
he could pay her back
if he mopped her floor
after school for five days.
"Okay," said Louis Jr.

"And then I'll help you with your reading," said Mabel.

"Cool!" said Jack.

"Cool!" said Louis Jr.

"Will he get cookies as rewards?" asked Jack.

"Of course," said Mabel.

"Lucky!" said Jack.

Bunny and Jack went home
with coupons for free tea anytime
at Mabel's Tea Room.

"I bet that igloo was tasty," said Jack.

"If you like glue," said Bunny.

"Well, I can put up with a lot,"
said Jack.
He tripped and knocked a plant
into Bunny's lap.

Bunny smiled.

"So can I, Jack," she said. "So can I."